The Thre

a

Jane C

WALKER BOOKS
AND SUBSIDIARIES
LONDON · BOSTON · SYDNEY

The Three Little Pigs

Once upon a time there was an old mother pig who had three little pigs. As she was too poor to keep them, she sent them out to seek their fortune.

The first little pig set off, and he met a man with a bundle of straw. "Please, Sir," said the first little pig, "give me that straw to build a house," which the man did, and the first little pig built his house.

No sooner had he finished
when along came a wolf
and knocked at the door.
"Little pig, little pig, let me
come in," said the wolf.
And the little pig answered,
"No, no, no! Not by the hair
of my chinny chin chin!"
So the wolf said,
"Then I'll huff
and I'll puff
and I'll *bloooow*
your house in!"

And the wolf huffed and he puffed and he blew
the house in, and ate up the
first little pig.

The second little pig met a
man with a bundle of sticks.
"Please, Sir," said the
second little pig, "give me
those sticks to build a house,"
which the man did, and the
second little pig built his house.
No sooner had he finished when along
came a wolf and knocked at the door.
"Little pig, little pig, let me come in," said
the wolf. And the little pig answered,
"No, no, no! Not by the hair
of my chinny chin chin!"
So the wolf said, "Then I'll huff and I'll
puff and I'll *bloooow* your house in!"

And the wolf huffed and he puffed,
and he *puffed* and he *huffed*, and
at last he blew the house in,
and ate up the second
little pig.

The third little pig met a
man with a load of bricks.
"Please, Sir," said the
third little pig, "give me
those bricks to build a house,"
which the man did, and the
third little pig built her house.
No sooner had she finished when along
came a wolf and knocked at the door.
"Little pig, little pig, let me come in,"
said the wolf. And the little pig answered,
"No, no, no! Not by the hair of my chinny
chin chin!"
So the wolf said, "Then I'll huff and
I'll puff and I'll *bloooow* your house in!"

And the wolf huffed and he puffed,
and he *puffed* and he *huffed*,
and he **huffed**
and he **puffed**,

but he could not blow the house in.

Then the wolf was very angry
indeed and said he would
come down the chimney
and eat up the little pig.
So the third little pig made
a blazing fire, and put a
huge pot of water on to
boil. Just as the wolf was
coming down the chimney,
the little pig took the lid
off the pot, and in fell
the wolf.
Then the little pig
put the lid back on again, boiled up the wolf until
nothing was left of him, and lived happily ever after.

Goldilocks and the Three Bears

Once upon a time there were three bears who all lived together in a little house in the forest. There was a great big Daddy Bear, a middle-sized Mummy Bear and a little tiny Baby Bear.

One morning the three bears made a pot of porridge for their breakfast, but it was too hot to eat.

"Let's go for a walk in the forest," said Mummy Bear. "When we get back, the porridge will have cooled."

Not long after the three bears
had left, a little girl with golden
hair came up to the house.
Her name was Goldilocks.
She knocked on the door
three times. When no one
answered, she tried the handle
and to her surprise the door opened.
Goldilocks walked in and went
straight over to the table.
"Oh, porridge! My favourite!"
she said.
First Goldilocks tasted the
porridge in the great big bowl.
"Ugh, much too salty!" she said.

Then she tasted the porridge in the middle-sized bowl. "Ooh, much too sweet!" she said.

Last of all she tasted the porridge in the tiny baby bowl. "Mmm, just right!" said Goldilocks and she ate it all up.

Goldilocks felt very full, so she went into the sitting-room, where there were three chairs. First she sat on the great big chair. "Ow, much too hard!" she said.

Then she sat on the middle-sized chair. "Ooh, much too soft!" she said.

Last of all she sat on the tiny baby chair. "Ahh, just right!" sighed Goldilocks.

But – CRACK! – the tiny baby chair broke into pieces and Goldilocks fell on to the floor.

Now Goldilocks felt tired.
She went upstairs to the
three bears' bedroom.
First she lay down on
the great big bed.
"Ooh, much too
high!" she said.

Then she lay down on the middle-sized bed.
"Ugh, much too lumpy!" she said.
Last of all she lay down
on the tiny baby bed.
"Ahh, just right!"
said Goldilocks
and she went
straight to sleep.

Soon the three bears came back from their walk.

They were all very hungry.

Daddy Bear looked at his great big bowl.

"Who's been eating *my* porridge?"

he said in his great

big voice.

Mummy Bear looked at her middle-sized bowl.
"Who's been eating *my* porridge?" she said
in her middle-sized voice.
Then Baby Bear looked
at his tiny baby bowl.
"Who's been eating
my porridge?" he cried
in his tiny baby voice.
"And has EATEN IT
ALL UP!"

The three bears went into the sitting-room. Daddy Bear turned around to sit in his chair. "Who's been sitting in *my* chair?" he said in his great big voice.

Mummy Bear looked
at her chair.
"Who's been sitting
in *my* chair?"
she said in her
middle-sized voice.
Then Baby Bear looked
at his chair.
"Who's been
sitting in my
chair?" he cried
in his tiny baby
voice. "And has
BROKEN IT
ALL TO BITS!"

The three bears ran upstairs to look in their bedroom.
"Who's been sleeping in *my* bed?" said Daddy Bear in his great big voice.
"Who's been sleeping in *my* bed?" said Mummy Bear in her middle-sized voice.
Then Baby Bear looked at his bed.
"Who's been sleeping in my bed?"

he cried in his tiny baby voice.

"And IS STILL THERE!"

Goldilocks woke up and was very frightened
to see the three bears all looking down at her.
She leaped out of bed, jumped straight out
of the window and ran
home as fast as
she could.

And the three bears never saw her again.

The Little Red Hen

Once upon a time there was a little red hen
who lived in a farmyard with a dog, a cat and
a goose. One day the little red hen found
some grains of wheat.

"Who will help me plant this wheat?" she asked.

"Not I!" said the dog.

"Not I!" said the cat.

"Not I!" said the goose.

"Then I shall plant it myself,"
said the little red hen.

And she did.

The wheat grew and grew and when summer
came, it turned golden yellow in the sun.
Now it was ready to be harvested.
"Who will help me cut this wheat?"
asked the little red hen.
"Not I!" said the dog.
"Not I!" said the cat.
"Not I!" said the goose.
"Then I shall cut it myself,"
said the little red hen.

And she did.

Now the wheat needed to be threshed,
to separate the hard husks from the grain.
"Who will help me thresh this wheat?"
asked the little red hen.
"Not I!" said the dog.
"Not I!" said the cat.
"Not I!" said the goose.
"Then I shall thresh it myself,"
said the little red hen.

And she did.

Now the grain was ready to go to the
mill, to be ground into flour.
"Who will help me carry this grain
to the mill?" asked the little red hen.
"Not I!" said the dog.
"Not I!" said the cat.
"Not I!" said the goose.
"Then I shall carry it myself,"
said the little red hen.

And she did.

The miller ground the grain into flour, ready for
baking and the little red hen carried it home.
"Who will help me bake this flour into bread?"
asked the little red hen.
"Not I!" said the dog.
"Not I!" said the cat.
"Not I!" said the goose.
"Then I shall bake it myself,"
said the little red hen.

And she did.

When the bread was baked to a golden brown,
the little red hen took it out of the oven.
A delicious smell drifted over the farmyard.
"Who will help me eat this bread?"
asked the little red hen.

"I will!" said the dog.

"I will!" said the cat.

"I will!" said the goose.

"Oh no, you won't!" said the little red hen.

"I shall eat it all myself!"

And she did . . .

right down to the very last crumb.

For Grandad

First published 1997 by Walker Books Ltd
87 Vauxhall Walk, London SE11 5HJ

This edition published 2002

2 4 6 8 10 9 7 5 3

Illustrations © 1997 Jane Chapman

Printed in Hong Kong

British Library Cataloguing in Publication Data:
a catalogue record for this book is
available from the British Library

ISBN 0-7445-8921-5